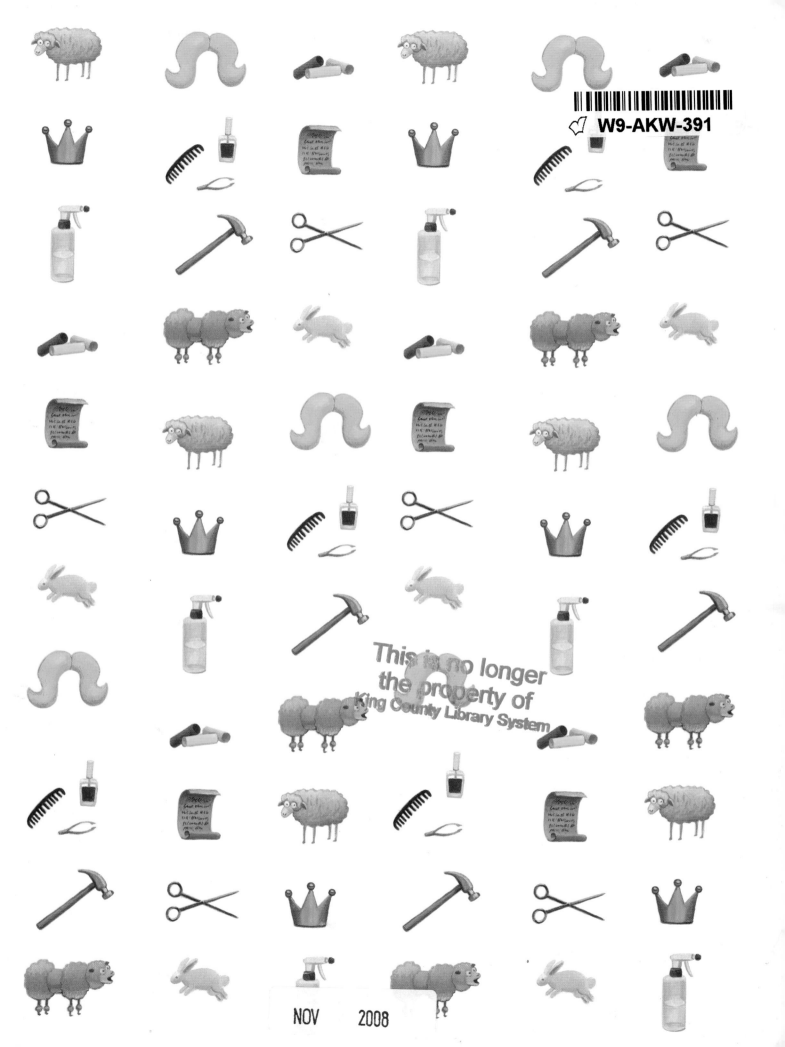

NOV   2008

For Diane, the inspiration; and for Alice, the best
—C.B.

DIAL BOOKS FOR YOUNG READERS
A division of Penguin Young Readers Group
Published by The Penguin Group
Penguin Group (USA) Inc., 375 Hudson Street, New York, NY 10014, U.S.A.
Penguin Group (Canada), 90 Eglinton Avenue East, Suite 700, Toronto, Ontario, Canada M4P 2Y3 (a division of
Pearson Penguin Canada Inc.) · Penguin Books Ltd, 80 Strand, London WC2R 0RL, England · Penguin Ireland, 25 St.
Stephen's Green, Dublin 2, Ireland (a division of Penguin Books Ltd) · Penguin Group (Australia), 250 Camberwell
Road, Camberwell, Victoria 3124, Australia (a division of Pearson Australia Group Pty Ltd) · Penguin Books India
Pvt Ltd, 11 Community Centre, Panchsheel Park, New Delhi - 110 017, India · Penguin Group (NZ), 67 Apollo Drive,
Rosedale, North Shore 0632, New Zealand (a division of Pearson New Zealand Ltd) · Penguin Books (South Africa)
(Pty) Ltd, 24 Sturdee Avenue, Rosebank, Johannesburg 2196, South Africa · Penguin Books Ltd, Registered Offices: 80
Strand, London WC2R 0RL, England

Text copyright © 2008 by Caralyn Buehner
Pictures copyright © 2008 by Mark Buehner
All rights reserved

The publisher does not have any control over and does not assume any responsibility for author or third-party websites
or their content. · Designed by Lily Malcom · Text set in Opti Worcester · Manufactured in China on acid-free paper
10 9 8 7 6 5 4 3 2 1

Library of Congress Cataloging-in-Publication Data

Buehner, Caralyn.
 The Queen of Style / by Caralyn Buehner ; pictures by Mark Buehner.
   p. cm.
 Summary: When a bored queen decides to take a beauty school
correspondence course, she begins monopolizing the time of her village's
farmers with practice sessions in hairdressing and nail care.
 ISBN: 978-0-8037-2878-3
 [1. Kings, queens, rulers, etc.—Fiction. 2. Beauty culture—Fiction.]
I. Buehner, Mark, ill. II. Title.
 PZ7.B884Qu 2008
 [E]—dc22
                  2007050702

The art was prepared by using oil paints over acrylics.

Readers, see if you can find a cat, a rabbit, and a Tyrannosaurus rex hidden in each picture.

The Queen of Style

by Caralyn Buehner

pictures by

Mark Buehner

Dial Books

for Young Readers

There once was a queen who ruled over a very small kingdom of farmers and sheep.

Every day the queen, whose name was Sophie, would sit on her throne and wait for someone to come in with a problem, if there was one, which there usually wasn't. The sheep were well-behaved, and so were the farmers. But Queen Sophie had nothing to do, and she was very bored.

Sophie called for the jester. "Amuse me," she commanded.

The jester did his best. Day after day he told jokes, juggled balls, or somersaulted, until there was nothing else he could think of to do. Then they were both bored.

"Can't you do something?" asked Queen Sophie.

"No," answered the jester crossly. "Can't you?"

The queen had to think about that.

"I don't know how to do anything except be the queen," she told the jester, as he packed his bags to leave.

"Then learn," he said shortly. "Good-bye."

Sophie thought and thought about what the jester had said. It would be nice
to be able to do something besides sit around and be queen. But what?
She searched through all her old message scrolls.

She pored over all of the books in the castle. She read the news-parchment.
And finally, one day, Sophie spotted an ad for something that seemed to be
just what she was looking for:

ROYAL COLLEGE OF BEAUTY

Correspondence Course

Learn the art of beautifying

in 12 easy lessons!

Amazing new styles

Exciting new looks!

Enroll now!

★

"I certainly will," said the queen, and she sent away for the lessons immediately.

Sophie was excited when the supplies from the beauty school arrived. She couldn't wait to get started! Every night she stayed up late studying the history of beautifying. She memorized directions for cutting, curling, coloring, and plucking. But there was one part of the course that had the queen stumped. She was supposed to practice each lesson fifty times, on fifty different people.

How would she ever do that? She didn't know fifty people. She wasn't even sure if there were fifty people in all her kingdom.

But there *were* people in her kingdom, and they would just have to help their queen.

Sophie wrote out a proclamation and tacked it up on every tree in the kingdom. It read:

When Sophie opened the castle doors the next morning, all of the people of the kingdom were there waiting.

"Right this way," the queen directed.

One by one she had each person sit down on a chair in the middle of the courtyard. She pinned a sheet around their necks and wet down their hair. Then she lifted up her shiny scissors, and slowly began to cut.

Chop. Chop. She cut the hair of all of the men. *Snip, snip.* She cut the hair of all of the women. *Chop, snip.* It was much harder to do than it had looked in the drawings. She cut the hair of all of the girls, and then the hair of all of the boys. When she was through cutting, the castle floor was covered in hair, but Queen Sophie was humming. She hadn't been bored once all day. She had enjoyed herself so much that she didn't want to stop. So she went outside and trimmed up all of the sheep.

A few days later, Sophie was ready to practice the next lesson. Again she rode around the kingdom tacking up notices on all of the trees.

Everyone come to the
Castle tomorrow
Queen's Orders
Bring your sheep too.

This time Queen Sophie curled the hair of everyone in the kingdom. She rolled and steamed the hair of all the men, women, boys, and girls, one by one. She didn't notice the grumbling of the men. She was too busy. And when she was finished with the people, she curled all of the wool of all of the sheep.

The next week the queen tacked up another notice. When everyone came, Sophie took them by the hand, one by one. She soaked and filed, buffed and painted, until everyone had been manicured to perfection. When she finished working on all of the farmers' fingernails, she went out to look at the sheep. It was difficult, but she managed to prettify their hooves—a little.

The queen was singing when she went to bed. She had never had such fun.

All through the summer Queen Sophie worked on her course. Every week she commanded her subjects to come to the palace.

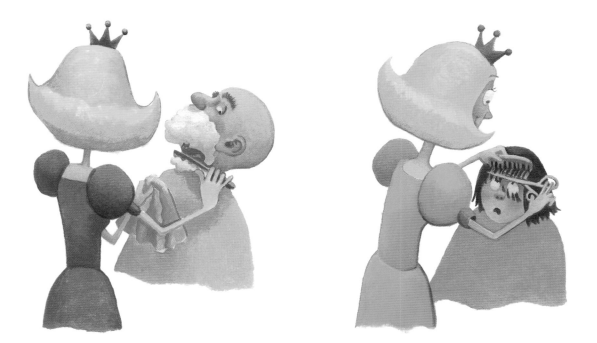

She shaved, shaped, colored, and waved. She steamed, conditioned, and waxed.

She tied ribbons and bows. When it was time to pluck, everyone in the kingdom had graceful, arching eyebrows (but she gave up on the sheep).

The queen had been working so hard that she almost didn't notice how much she had learned. She hardly realized that she had developed a flair for style. She spent all of her time studying for her final exam. She tacked up new commands on the trees almost daily.

One morning Queen Sophie could hear the rumble of voices outside before she even opened the castle doors. All of her subjects were gathered, and they did not look happy.

"Yes?" the queen asked sweetly. "Is there a problem?"

It took some time for the crowd to quiet enough for anyone to be heard. Then a large, burly man stepped forward.

"The problem we have, Your Majesty, is *you*. I don't want to come to the castle every other day to have my eyelashes dyed or my hair curled. I've got sheep to tend."

"That's right," called a woman. "I've got no need to have my chin shaved. I need to be spinning my wool."

Another farmer spoke up. "And I would like my sheep to look like sheep!"

Sophie was devastated. She had been having so much fun that she hadn't noticed that the others were not. She was very quiet as they complained, one by one. When the crowd fell silent, the queen finally spoke.

"I'm sorry," she said softly. "You don't have to come here anymore. I didn't mean to bother you. I guess I thought you were enjoying everything as much as I was."

The people looked at one another. Then the big farmer stepped forward again.

"I don't like curling," he said. "But I do like my beard trimmed."

"And I like to have my hair dyed red," shouted a woman in the back of the crowd.

Then the others began to call out. "I want my nails done!" "I like to have me hair curled." "I'd like a shave, now and again." "The children could use a haircut, now that summer's well on." "My George has never looked so good!" "I *did* like the smell of my sheep with that fancy shampoo."

The queen looked at the farmers standing there. *Her* farmers. She thought about how they had come to the castle day after day, rain or shine. Really, it was remarkable how patient they had been.

"From this time forth," Queen Sophie proclaimed, "just come to the castle when *you* want to. I promise that from now on, I will do *your* bidding."

Then one day there was a letter on everyone's doorstep. It read:

I'm finally graduating — Yes, it's true!
I'm glad for all I've learned to do.
Couldn't have made it through without you.
Come to my party and bring your sheep too!

The party was a great success. As Queen Sophie circulated around the courtyard with a tray of dainty sandwiches, she realized that she had gained something more important than a license as a beautician. She had friends.

She knew that Jack liked his hair long, and that Suzanna preferred the lavender-

scented shampoo. She knew who was expecting a baby, whose grandmother had been sick, and who was visiting from out of town. She had gotten to know each sheep too. She had almost forgotten about being queen. It didn't really seem very important anymore.

The farmers didn't forget. They were proud when they went to market with their beautiful wives and handsome children.

But it was the spectacular sheep that brought real fame to Sophie, who became known from kingdom to kingdom ever after as the Queen of Style.